JUMP

Jump
by Fanie Viljoen

Published by Ransom Publishing Ltd.
Radley House, 8 St. Cross Road, Winchester, Hampshire SO23 9HX, UK
www.ransom.co.uk

ISBN   978 178127 659 4
First published in Afrikaans in 2014
This English edition first published in 2015

JUMP

Fanie Viljoen

Ransom

1

Happy birthday, dear Rudi

'It's brilliant!' cried Rudi.

'More than brilliant!' cried Liz.

'Oh, please!' sighed Steven. He lay stretched out on Rudi's bed. His hand behind his head. 'It's only a video camera. Even simple mobile phones can shoot videos.'

'But not like this one.'

Rudi stroked the camera. His fingers lightly

touching the buttons. He unfolded the small screen. 'I've always wanted one.'

'Oh, please,' Steven called out again. He shook his head. 'Get over it, will you? It's not as if you've found a girl.'

Everybody knew Rudi was struggling to find a girl.

Rudi didn't know why he had so much trouble.

With girls.

It was supposed to be easy. He was a cool guy. Not even bad looking, he thought.

Perhaps it was the dimple in his cheek. It made him look like a mommy's boy.

Or perhaps he had bad breath. And nobody told him.

Perhaps he just didn't understand girls. They could be very strange.

Rudi shifted his gaze to his friend, Lizz.

She was kind of cute: slim body, black hair … She wanted to get a tattoo on her shoulder.

She showed him a picture of it once:

But her mom refused.

Even Rudi didn't like the idea.

She had a super silky skin. A tattoo would only spoil it.

Rudi smiled. He would love to slip his hand over her shoulder one day. Perhaps kiss her skin …

But that would never happen.

Lizz wasn't interested in Rudi. She was into tough guys. Rudi was too tame for her liking.

Okay, he did have a few muscles. He got them from playing rugby.

What he also got was a bloody nose once. And he only cried very, VERY softly.

But other than that he was just a normal bloke.

At least Lizz and he were still friends. Ordinary guys make for good friends.

'Happy birthday,' said Lizz.

It shook Rudi out of his daydream.

Lizz wrapped a few streamers around Rudi's head. Then she tied a silver balloon to his shirt button.

Rudi laughed. He liked it when she touched him. But he didn't want to show it. So he asked: 'What are you doing, Lizz?'

'I'm wishing you well!' she answered playfully.

'No, wait,' said Rudi, stopping her.

He switched on the camera. Then he aimed it at her. The image on the small screen was bumpy at first. Then it fell into focus.

'Okay, Lizz, say that again.'

Steven rolled his eyes, irritated. And looked away.

'Happy birthday, old Rudi!' Lizz cried out.
She posed for the camera.
Her smile looked just like Paris Hilton's.

What's up with Steven?

That evening Rudi was sitting watching TV
till very late.

His parents had already gone to bed.

Next to him on the couch was a small side
plate. And a dried-out slice of birthday cake.
He'd already had three slices. And some
custard tart. And blueberry tart.

Rudi grinned. Luckily one's birthday only

came once a year. He would have to shake the extra weight off during rugby training. A fly half should be fleet of foot.

Steven said Rudi has wings on his feet. That's how it feels when Rudi is heading for the try line. When he knows nothing will stop him now.

It was a pity Lizz didn't like rugby heroes. They weren't her style.

Rudi's thoughts suddenly shifted back to Steven. His pal acted a bit strangely today. What was wrong with him?

Rudi picked up his mobile phone.

He sent a message to Lizz.

WHAT WAS WRONG WITH STEVEN TODAY???

Her reply came shortly after:

STEVEN IS JEALOUS. DON'T WORRY. SLEEP TIGHT, B-DAY BOY!

Rudi nodded, deep in thought. She was probably right. Steven's parents aren't well off. He'll probably never receive a huge gift on his birthday.

The plan

The following day Steven was in a better mood.

He first paid a visit to Rudi's fridge.

'I'm as hungry as a wolf,' he complained.

He helped himself to some leftover cake.

A HUGE helping.

Rudi was sick of cake. He poured them some soft drinks.

Then they went outside. Steven collapsed in a garden chair.

'Where's that camera of yours, old Rudi?'

'Why?' Rudi asked warily.

'We should try it out.'

'I did.'

'No, dude,' said Steven. 'That's not what I meant. I think we should make a cool video.'

'Of what?'

'I don't know – of stuff.'

'*Stuff* doesn't make good videos, Steven,' said Rudi. '*Ideas* make good videos.'

'Then we should think of a good idea.' Steven gulped down some more cake. A dreamy expression played in his eyes. 'Where's Lily today?'

'I don't know. Around. She's probably hanging out in the shade. Near the fish pond, reading. Why?'

'I haven't yet said hello to her today.'

Rudi frowned. 'I don't understand. Were you supposed to? You came to visit *me*.'

Steven sighed. 'Never mind, forget it.'

Rudi shook his head. Strange. Since when was Steven interested in his sister?

'I've got an idea,' said Steven. He wiped up the last few cake crumbs with his finger.

'What now?'

'For the video, man.' Steven put the plate down. He stuck his hand in his pocket. And pulled out a bunch of red fire-crackers.

'What? Fire-crackers? Are you ten years old again? You aren't allowed to set those things off here,' said Rudi.

Steven pretended not to hear Rudi. His eyes shone. 'I think we ought to.'

'Is *that* your wonderful idea for a video?' asked Rudi.

Steven dangled the string of fire-crackers in front of Rudi's face. 'No, that's not all … We are going to scare Lily with them!'

Revenge

'I don't know,' said Rudi. 'Lily would be furious.'

'And rightly so,' said Steven. 'But she would laugh her head off afterwards.'

'And the video?' asked Rudi. 'Where does it fit in with your brilliant idea?'

'Come on, Rudi,' said Steven, shaking his head. 'Some days you're as stupid as mud. We frighten her with the fire-crackers. And we tape everything with the video camera.'

'And then?' asked Rudi.

'Then we upload it to YouTube!'

'Lily would definitely hate that,' laughed Rudi.

'She would *love* it!' cried Steven. 'You'll see. Your sister has a good sense of humour.'

'But the whole wide world will see it!'

'Exactly!' cried Steven. 'We are going to make her famous. World famous.'

Rudi didn't know why he was even considering it. It was a bad idea. A very bad idea. The kind of plan Steven would typically use to impress a girl. The kind of plan that never worked.

But then he recalled the previous week. Lily had gotten hold of his Facebook password. It was written on his rugby calendar. And she had used it!

The guys at school had a field day with him. Boy, did they laugh! Some still question his love for knitting and crochet work. And why *Winnie the Pooh* is his favourite book.

There were also those terrible photos she uploaded of him as a young lad.

But worst of all: he'd been Facebook friends with the All Blacks' rugby captain for a few days! He hated the All Blacks!

'So, are you in or out?' asked Steven.

Rudi smiled. 'Do you have something to light the crackers?'

Fireworks!

Steven carefully explained the plan to Rudi:

1. Rudi would hide behind the vines in the garden. From there he would be able to see everything. But Lily wouldn't be able to see him.
2. Rudi would switch on the camera. He would record everything.
3. Steven would sneak through the garden.

Lily wouldn't see him if he approached from behind.

4. At the herb garden he would have to be extra careful.

5. At the rose garden he would have to be extra, *extra* careful.

6. When reaching the fish pond, he would light the fire-crackers.

7. He would then throw the crackers. They would land on the paving. Right in front of the garden bench where Lily sat reading.

8. Lily would get the fright of her life.

9. She would run straight into Steven – her hero's – arms.

10. She would immediately fall madly in love with him.

11. They would live happily ever after.

The end.

Okay, that's not really how Steven explained it.

Steps 9, 10 and 11 were totally different:

9. Lily would make a few funny moves with her arms.
10. She might even jump up and down on the garden bench. Anything hilarious would be fantastic.
11. They upload the video to YouTube.

That was the plan.

But that was not what happened.

Rudi watched as Steven slipped the fire-crackers in his pocket. Then the lighter.

He was glad his parents weren't home. This whole affair could land him in serious trouble.

Steven rubbed his hands together. He cracked his knuckles. Rudi didn't know why. He wasn't going to a fight!

Steven gave a confident smile. He showed Rudi the thumbs up.

Rudi switched on the video camera.

'Are you ready?' asked Steven.

Rudi nodded. He turned the camera on himself first.

'Guys and girls,' he announced. 'Are you ready for some fireworks? My pal, Steven, plans on giving my sister, Lily, the fright of her life. I reckon he is looking for trouble. Or attention. We will just have to wait and see what happens. Don't try this with your sister. Steven is a real idiot.'

Rudi smiled broadly.

'Let's check it out … '

He turned the camera on Steven. Steven gave a maniacal laugh. Then he dashed off, away from the camera.

The camera followed him as he zigzagged through the garden. Past this bush, around that tree. He was like the hero in a video game.

Or like a guy who wished he was the hero in a video game.

For a second the camera angle shifted to

Lily. She was still oblivious. She kept on reading.

Then Steven was back in view again.

He tiptoed past the herb garden. A thumbs up sign showed he was still okay.

Then onwards.

Slowly.

Softly …

Past the rose bushes.

Now both Steven and Lily appeared on screen. Lily had still not heard or seen anything. She turned the page.

Steven sneaked off to the reed bush.

He removed the fire-crackers from his pocket.

Using the lighter he struck up a small flame.

It died in the breeze.

'Idiot!' whispered Rudi softly. He laughed.

Steven tried again.

Everything was going according to plan …

The crackers' fuse lit up.

Steven smiled broadly.

Three.

Two.

One.

Steven raised his hand.

He tossed the fire-crackers forward.

No!

Something was wrong.

One of the fire-crackers in the bunch caught. On Steven's watch!

The first crackers went off.

Lily jumped to her feet. She stared back over her shoulder.

She wasn't startled.

She was laughing.

Steven was the one filled with terror.

He wasn't laughing.

He threw his hands in the air. His arms swung about wildly. But the string of crackers was still stuck.

His eyes were wide.

The fire-crackers were banging, banging, banging around his arm.

Steven tried to stop them. Smacking at them furiously.

Not watching his step at all.

And then it happened.

Rudi watched in horror as Steven tumbled into the fish pond.

The water – and a few koi fish – splashed over the side.

Steven tried getting to his feet again. But the bottom of the fish pond was slimy. His feet slipped out from under him. More water and fish splashed out of the pond.

At long last the final fire-cracker died with a hiss.

But there had been fireworks.

Just as Rudi had promised.

Hits and misses

'You guys are crazy,' said Lizz at school. She dropped her bag next to theirs. A strange smile appeared on her face.

Luckily Steven had recovered from the shock. 'Did you see the video?' he asked.

'I did … and the rest of the country as well, probably,' she answered.

'The rest of the world!' boasted Rudi. He

couldn't believe Steven still uploaded the video. His plan ended in a total fiasco!

Steven gave a satisfied smile.

'YouTube is wonderful,' he sighed. 'It makes stars of ordinary people … '

He scratched around in his pocket and fished out his mobile phone. He opened the YouTube app. 'Look at that … 384,123 hits. Only 145 people weren't impressed.'

'My mom is one of them,' said Rudi.

'Your mom isn't my target audience.' Steven sighed happily. 'Hey, but what did Lily say?'

'Lily thinks you're a nutcase,' answered Rudi.

Steven grinned as if it was a huge compliment. 'But did she like the video?'

'Duh!?' cried Liz. 'You planned to blow her up with fire-crackers. Do you *think* she liked your video?'

Steven's grin was broader.

'I'm very lucky I wasn't grounded,' said Rudi. 'My mom hates fire-crackers. It upsets the dogs. You know how much she loves animals.'

'Aah, sweet!' said Lizz. She put her arm around Rudi's shoulder and gave him a quick hug. His cheeks turned red immediately. Within a second the glow had spread throughout his body. It felt amazing.

Then Lizz leaned over Rudi. She snatched the mobile phone. Again she watched the YouTube video. 'Cool comments, aren't they?' she said.

'My fans … ' replied Steven with pride.

'Hey, guys, check this out … ' said Lizz after a while. 'One of your fans wants to meet you. His name is Marco. He lives in the neighbourhood.'

Marco …

The name sent a chill down Rudi's spine. He couldn't explain why.

Marco = trouble?

'I think he's here,' said Liz. She sounded very excited.

Rudi stared out the window. A shiny motorbike stood in the driveway.

A guy dressed in black leather got off. He was about Rudi's age. He removed the helmet and checked himself in the rear-view mirror. Then he drew his fingers through his dark hair.

'Sexy … ' whispered Lizz.

Rudi stared at her anxiously. He didn't need competition. Had she already fallen for Marco? She hadn't even met him yet!

'He looks kind of rough,' said Steven.

'Exactly what I like … ' said Lizz. Light-footed she hurried to the front door.

Girls! thought Rudi. He felt annoyed.

Marco approached the house with a cool swagger.

Rudi didn't want to judge people. But something told him: Trouble was on the way.

'Don't you have anything stronger?' asked Marco. He took the glass of Coke Rudi held out to him.

Lizz laughed. She sat down next to Marco. *Too close*, thought Rudi.

'Rudi drinks nothing stronger than soft drinks,' said Lizz.

Rudi wished he could spill some Coke on

her. Why did she say that? Was she trying to impress Marco?

Rudi decided to keep his mouth shut.

It was clear she had fallen under Marco's spell. Enchanted by his swagger. His deep voice. His cool, lazy way of talking.

Steven pulled a face. He probably noticed it too.

At first the conversation centred around school. Marco was in a neighbouring school from the one Rudi and his friends attended.

'I'm in Gorge High,' he said. 'Not that I attend very often. You know what I mean?'

He grinned, taking a sip of soft drink.

Rudi frowned.

'I liked your video,' said Marco. He turned to Steven. 'It was quite funky. You're very talented, Steven.'

Steven pushed his chest out slightly. He seemed pleased.

What? thought Rudi. It was a hilarious video, but *talent*? Steven set off some fire-crackers.

And ended up in a fish pond. It was more stupidity than talent.

'I think you could do more,' said Marco. 'Do better … ' Danger hid in his voice.

Lizz made giddy noises.

'I can help you,' said Marco. He gave a chilling smile. 'I've got loads of ideas!'

A hundred metres of madness

Steven bit down on a block of ice. Shards of it shot from his mouth. He couldn't contain his excitement.

'Better?' he asked. His eyes were wide. 'I can do better! I can frighten somebody else with fire-crackers. More crackers. Perhaps a cop or somebody!'

Marco shook his head. He got up,

approaching confidently. He placed his hands on Steven's shoulders. And looked him straight in the eye.

'No, Steven. That isn't really what I had in mind,' said Marco. 'You're not thinking big enough.'

Steven frowned.

'You did the fire-cracker thing. The next video should take things a step further ... '

'You mean like rockets?' Steven asked. He sounded unsure.

Marco shook his head.

Rudi didn't want to know what was to follow.

'Something completely different. Something crazy!' said Marco. 'I think you should run the hundred metres.'

'I can do that,' said Steven. 'I'm quite fast. But that isn't crazy ... '

'Yes, but you are going to do it barefoot ... on a track laden with mouse traps ... '

'Wha-a-at?' cried Steven.

Marco seemed pleased. 'It's a good idea. It might hurt, but it sounds like loads of fun. That's something *I'd* watch on YouTube. Other people will too.'

Rudi could see Steven was considering the proposal. He wasn't really going to do it … was he?

'Okay!' cried Steven. 'Where will we find enough mouse traps for a hundred metres of total madness?'

'Ouch, damn!'

'Is he crazy?'

'Auuuw!'

These were the words Rudi heard most of all. The whole school knew about the new video.

And Steven and his friends received a new name: the Vidiots.

Rudi wasn't sure he liked the name.

He also wasn't sure why he was considered as one of the Vidiots.

He was merely the cameraman.

He didn't even *like* the job. He didn't like being in Marco's company. Marco was something of a slime ball.

But Steven kept on nagging. Until he agreed.

'Did you seen the Vidiots?'

At first Rudi thought the girl was speaking to him, but she was talking to a friend. Another one joined them. They huddled together around the mobile phone.

They were watching the new video.

Rudi heard Marco encouraging Steven:

'Come on, Steven. Run! Get your knees up, bro!'

Steven sounded like a cat on a hot tin roof.

He moaned and groaned terribly.

Eventually the mousetraps stopped snapping.

But Steven was still swearing.

Rudi knew what was to happen next – a close-up: Steven's red toes filling the screen.

A mousetrap hanging from every second toe.

Always one step further

Steven was a SUPERSTAR!

Or so he thought.

Rudi couldn't believe it. It was only a video about mousetraps. And somebody crazy enough to dash over them.

But Rudi couldn't argue. Everybody was watching the video on YouTube. It spread like a virus.

The links to the video was everywhere: on Facebook, Twitter …

'Why are you so quiet?' Rudi's mom asked. They were in a shopping mall. It was very busy.

'I'm thinking,' he answered.

'Oh, should I be worried? Is it about school? Girls?'

Rudi smiled. 'No, Mom! It's Steven. And the videos.'

'You should be careful,' she said. 'I'm not racing to a hospital because of a silly video.'

'You know I'm always careful, Mom.'

She gave his hand a little squeeze. He winked at her. Smiled.

'I'm off to the music shop,' said Rudi, before his mom could ask any more questions. 'I'll meet you there. I want to buy Hot Head's new CD.'

Hot Head was Rudi's favourite indie band. He had all their CDs.

That was something he and Lizz had in

common. They both liked Hot Head's music.

One of these days he would get to see the band play live. They were booked for the school's annual rock concert. Rudi couldn't wait.

As he made his way to the CD shop, a text message arrived. He pulled his phone from his pocket.

The message was from Marco.

500,000 HITS! THE NEXT ONE WILL BE CRAZIER.

Rudi didn't know if he should be happy. Perhaps.

Marco's words from that very first day came back to him: *The next video should take things a step further …*

It made Rudi uncomfortable.

Every video would be more dangerous than the previous one.

Today fire-crackers …

Tomorrow mousetraps …
Then … what?

What's inside the box?

'Isn't Lily with you?' asked Steven.

'What?' asked Rudi.

He came strolling across the school's empty parking bay. It was a Saturday afternoon. They were to meet Marco there.

'Lily. Your sister!' Steven tried again. 'I thought she would join you. To come and watch, you know.'

'You leave my sister alone, Steven,' protested Rudi. 'I can see what's going on. You think she likes you. Or you *think* she will like you if she sees the weird stuff you get up to. But she's not that kind of girl. Forget about her.'

'But … '

'But nothing!' Rudi said decidedly. 'If you two should ever hook up, it will mess with our friendship.'

Steven ruffled his wild hair. He seemed a bit peeved. But Rudi didn't care. He was glad Steven knew how he felt.

Rudi fiddled with his video camera. He wasn't in the mood to make another video. But he was doing it for Steven.

And to ensure that Lizz and Marco didn't get too friendly with each other …

Marco headed their way. He carried a glass cage and a box.

'What are we doing today?' asked Steven.

'You're quite nosey!' said Marco. He put the

glass cage and box down. He gave Steven a sideways glace. Then he smiled slyly.

'Are you ready for your next video, guys?' He indicated to the box. It was made of stiff brown cardboard. The word *DANGER!* was written on the side.

Marco drummed his fingers on the lid.

Something moved inside …

Rudi shot a scared-looking glance at Steven.

What was inside the box?

Marco got hold of the lid.

He raised it …

Slowly.

Then Rudi and Steven saw …

In the darkened belly of the box, a snake lay, all curled up.

Sturdy body. Orange scales with dark circles along the back. About a metre long.

Steven watched in horror. 'Is the thing poisonous?' he asked.

'Who knows,' said Marco. 'We'll find out soon enough … '

'What?' cried Rudi and Steven.

'Did Marco tell you about the next video?' Lizz shouted from a distance. She came running, a skateboard in her hands.

Rudi's heart missed a beat. *Damn, she was pretty. That smile … It could melt an iceberg.*

Rudi pulled himself together.

He stared down at the skateboard. 'And this?'

'It's my brother's,' said Lizz. 'But you may borrow it for the video. Will you also be making an appearance on camera today, Rudi?'

'No thanks,' he said firmly. 'I feel much safer behind the scenes.'

Lizz laughed. She probably thought he was a sissy. But Rudi didn't care. He didn't know what Marco had planned. Whatever it was – he was glad he didn't have to do it.

Lizz fell in beside Marco. She placed her hand around his waist. He kissed her on the forehead.

Rudi felt sick. Because of this video thing …
and for Lizz and Marco's sake. She had fallen
head over heels in love with him.

Damn Marco!

'Today you're going to jump over the snake
with a skateboard, Steven.'

Marco said it as if it was dead easy. 'The glass
box will give us a better view of the snake. That's
real scary. See how pale Rudi is already … '

Is Marco ridiculing him? wondered Rudi. He
didn't do a thing about it, but he thought: *The
piece of filth.*

'People would love it,' Marco carried on.

'I can't ride a skateboard,' Steven said softly.

'Even better!' cried Marco. 'People want to
see ordinary guys do extraordinary stuff.'

'I don't know,' said Steven.

'You don't have to if you don't want to,'
Rudi said to Steven. He was also worried. It
sounded very dangerous.

'Don't listen to the party pooper, Steven,'
said Marco.

Party pooper! Rudi was getting angry again.

Marco placed his hands on Steven's shoulders. He stared him straight in the eyes.

'Think about your fans. The Vidiots are a big hit. And it is going to get bigger.'

Marco gave the words time to sink in.

Then he added: 'You're not scared, are you, Steven?'

Trouble

The trick went wrong. Terribly wrong.

Rudi was shaking when it happened. He couldn't believe it. He tried to keep the camera steady.

Then he thought: *Forget the video. Go and help your pal!*

Steven's cries echoed against the school buildings.

Rudi put the camera down. Almost too hard.

'Are you okay, Steven?' cried Rudi as he ran closer.

He kicked the stuff they'd used for the ramp out of his way. The floorboards and bricks shifted over the concrete floor.

The skateboard was now lying to the side.

The ground lay covered in pieces of glass from the cage.

Steven crawled away from the snake.

Startled, it curled up on the concrete. It's mouth open. Black eyes flashing. It didn't seem as if it was hurt. But it wasn't happy.

In his head Rudi replayed everything. The training run was okay. But they didn't use the snake then. The second try was a nightmare.

Steven's forehead gleamed with sweat.

Marco announced the video.

He was full of bravado.

He asked if Steven was ready.

Steven dropped his head.

He gathered his courage.

Then he pushed off.

Everything happened so fast.

He struck the ramp.

At an angle, not straight like in the training run.

Arms and legs waving.

The skateboard tipped.

The floorboards shifted off the bricks.

Steven flew.

Steven fell.

The cage broke.

The snake underneath him ...

'Oh, don't make such a scene,' said Marco. 'It was incredible! You were incredible, Steven!'

Rudi helped his friend up. There was blood on his elbow. More blood streamed down his arm.

Marco picked the snake up. He caressed its scaly body. It made hissing noises.

He held the snake's head beside his own. He positioned it for Rudi and Steven to see. Pretending to be the snake, he whispered: 'I'm just a little old corn snake. I won't bite you, Steven. I strangle my pray … and I only eat rats … '

Drowning in Old Spice

The next Monday, before school, Rudi was waiting for Lizz to arrive. He needed to talk to her alone. Some place where Marco wasn't present.

'Can I have a word?' he asked when she finally came.

She nodded. He took her to a quiet place. The staircase near the library.

'What's up, Rudi?' asked Lizz. 'Is something bothering you?'

Rudi sighed heavily. 'I don't know why you're hooking up with him, Lizz.' His voice was cold.

'Who?'

'Marco. That weirdo with the black motorbike.'

'He isn't a weirdo,' snapped Lizz.

'What do you see in him?'

'Why? Are you jealous?'

'I'm just saying, Lizz. That guy is rubbish. I've finished with him.'

'I'm not. I like him, okay, Rudi?' She crossed her arms. 'You don't understand him. He is a great guy. He cares for me. Not like the other boyfriends I've had.'

I'll also care for you. But you have to give me a chance, Liz, thought Rudi.

His heart felt crushed.

He couldn't say it.

'Watch out for him, Liz,' Rudi said

eventually. 'He's as slippery as that snake of his.'

'Don't worry. I'm a big girl, Rudi. I can look after myself.' She gave a quick laugh. 'It is sweet of you to worry. You're like a big brother …'

Rudi shook his head. He didn't want to be her brother. He wanted …

'Look who's coming,' Lizz cried suddenly.

Steven was approaching. He playfully threw his arms wide open. 'Autographs later, people. Let me get the load off first!'

Lizz made room next to her. 'How is your arm? It looked kind of sore.'

'Oh, I'll live,' sighed Steven. He plopped down alongside her.

A cloud of aftershave hung around him.

'Phew!' choked Lizz. She pinched her nose.

Rudi also pulled a face. 'What's this, buddy? Had a dip in your dad's Old Spice?'

'Gross,' said Lizz. 'Who still wears Old Spice today? It's *so* last century!'

Steven just smiled. Rudi and Lizz's words didn't bother him. 'I'm doing it for the girls,' he said in a mysterious manner.

'Do you want to gas them?' Lizz asked.

'No, I want to blow them away!'

'Well, it works. You blew us away … but not in a good sense.' Lizz let go of her nose, gasping for breath.

'Well, I have good news today. Good news and VERY good news,' said Steven.

'Oh dear,' sighed Rudi.

As if announcing a wrestling match, Steven let it rip: 'First the good news. I'm completely over your sister, Rudi,' he said. 'There are many fish in the sea. That is where the VERY good news comes in. You should see! All the girls are checking me out.'

'Really?' asked Rudi.

'Yes! It's all because of those videos. I was mad at Marco for that last video. But you should see what the girls are writing on YouTube.'

'Oh, no!' Rudi sighed again. He could see where this conversation was heading.

'They think I'm sexy!' Steven pushed his chest out. 'Sexy with a capital S!'

'Well, what do you know!' laughed Lizz. 'And if they could smell you, they would reckon you stink. Stink with a capital S!'

Friends you can do without

HEY BRO, I'VE GOT ANOTHER GREAT IDEA FOR A VIDEO. PHONE ME.

WHY SO QUIET? I'VE GOT A CRAZY PLAN FOR VIDIOTS VIDEO. PHONE ME.

WHAT'S UP? BRO???

Marco was now sending Rudi a message every day.

Marco even went to Rudi's home. He hammered on the door. But Rudi didn't open it.

He didn't care what Marco thought. Why would he? He didn't need his friendship.

The Vidiots was now a thing of the past for him.

It had been a bad idea from the start.

From now on he would make videos of other stuff.

Safer stuff like …

The swimming pool?

Orange juice?

The book case?

The pimples on his face?

Rudi groaned. That again was too boring.

He stared at his camera.

The battery was dead. He didn't even care to charge it.

Rudi shook his head.

Perhaps it wasn't such a great present after all. He should've rather asked his parents for a PlayStation.

The rock concert

The sports grounds were already thundering when Rudi arrived. The rock concert was an annual event. A fund-raiser, the principal called it. Many of the teachers were on duty, but it was still fantastic.

The bands for the evening were:
Mortuary
Lost Child

Forgive Me
Hot Head
Zombie.

Hot Head was Rudi's favourite. Zombie was a close second. They seemed dangerous with their scary masks. And they sang about creepy stuff. Rudi wondered if the principal knew.

'*There* you are!' cried Steven above the music. 'I was looking everywhere.'

Rudi gave Steven a light sniff. Steven didn't go overboard with the Old Spice again.

But something else was odd …

'And that T-shirt?' asked Rudi. He frowned.

Steven had on a white T-shirt. A life-sized picture of his own face was printed on it. An ignited fuse curled above his head. As if it was a fire-cracker. And to top it all, the word:

VITIODS

'Wrong spelling. You switched the 't' and the 'd',' said Rudi.

'Huh?' groaned Steven. He swore under his breath. The loud music drowned it.

'Oh, Steven … ' was all Rudi could say.

'Did you bring your camera?' asked Steven, the spelling error forgotten.

'Why?'

'We're going to shoot another video, Rudi. Here! Tonight!' Steven was shaking with excitement.

'Is it one of Marco's clever ideas again?' asked Rudi.

Steven nodded. His eyes shone brightly. 'That's why I had the shirt made.'

'What are you going to do?'

'Wait till later, Rudi … you'll see.'

Lose your pain

The music got louder as the evening progressed. Hot Head sang Rudi's favourite song, 'Lose it'.

> *Lose your pain!*
> *Lose your fear!*
> *Stand strong*
> *Intentions clear!*
> *Never doubt, never dread*

For those secret worries
Are only in your head.

Rudi sang every word with the band. He tried to enjoy the evening. But it wasn't that easy.

He wished Steven and Lizz were there with him now. They always had a great time together.

That had all changed when Marco came along.

He wondered what Steven and Marco were up to.

And he wondered about Lizz. Was she even at the concert?

Rudi decided to go look for her.

There were so many kids around.

Empty glasses lay everywhere. The plastic cracked below his sneakers.

'You're the Vidiots' cameraman, aren't you?' one of the girls asked Rudi. 'I heard you're going to do something wild tonight. Please tell us what!'

'I don't know,' said Rudi in passing.
'Just give us a clue!' she cried after him.
Rudi didn't pay her any mind.
That's when he saw Lizz.
She was with Marco.
They were in each other's arms.
Kissing …

Embrace your pain

Rudi's life felt like it was coming to an end. His chest was almost tearing open.

Lose your pain! Again he heard Hot Head's words.

They didn't know what they were talking about. One can't simply *lose* one's pain.

It stays with you.

Perhaps even for always.

Rudi's lip started trembling. He bit down on it. He wasn't going to stand there and cry – even though he wanted to.

Embrace your pain!
Embrace your fear!
You're as weak
As you appear!

He changed the words to Hot Head's song to suit him.

For one last time he gazed back at Lizz. He still couldn't believe it. They looked like they were going to swallow each other.

He turned around.

Embrace your pain!

The anger still brewed inside him.

Embrace your fear!

He wished he could do something to Marco. He wanted to hurt him. But that was all talk. He wasn't that kind of guy.

Maybe, he thought, *it was time for a change. Perhaps he should become that kind of guy …*

Always doubt, always dread

For those secret worries
Are not only in your head.

Rudi sang the words over and over.

Would he be able to do it? Would he be able to put Marco in his place?

He was still thinking about it when he heard Marco. His voice was coming from the stage. It thundered through the speakers and carried across the field.

'Hey, guys and girls. Tonight is a very special night.'

Ignore him, thought Rudi. *Keep walking. Just get away.*

'We've got a live Vidiots show for you. Steven is here tonight.' A bunch of girls screamed. 'And he is beyond crazy!'

Rudi slowed down.

'Unfortunately our cameraman deserted us. But you all have mobile phones, right?' A bunch of guys whistled. Girls cheered. 'Tonight *you* are going to shoot the videos. And *you* are going to upload them to YouTube!'

Rudi stopped. What was Marco doing?

'You've heard of stage diving, right?' asked Marco.

'YES!' everybody screamed.

'The Vidiots will be taking it a step further tonight … Now, please turn your attention, and your cameras, to Steven!'

Rudi turned around.

His heart missed a beat.

His eyes followed Marco's pointing hand to the stage rigging. And right on top of it, high above the stage, was Steven. He stood there, arms stretched out to the side.

He was getting ready to jump …

Jump! Jump! Jump!

Rudi's body turned cold.

'No!' he whispered. Then louder: 'No! Steven, are you mad?'

Rudi went into action. Moving back to the stage.

The voices in the crowd rose above the music.

Mobile phone screens shone everywhere.

Ready to record Steven's dive.

Perhaps his death …

Fear filled every corner of Rudi's body.

It was yet another one of Marco's plans. He didn't care for anybody. That's why he came up with this stuff. It was all just one big joke to him.

But Steven was Rudi's pal. He had to stop him.

'Jump, jump, jump,' cried the guys and girls.

'No!' Rudi shouted again. 'Steven, get off there!'

But Steven would not be able to hear him above the noise.

Rudi watched as Steven shifted his gaze downwards. His body leaned forward gently. Then back. He wiped his hands on his trousers. A spotlight wiped over him.

Some of the teachers also tried getting him down now.

Rudi forced his way through the crowd.

They jostled against him. Bumped into him. Mobile phone cameras were everywhere.

'Steven, get down!'

Rudi didn't know if Steven saw him. For a second it seemed like he did. But from up there he was probably just one in a sea of faces.

'Steven! Don't be stupid!' cried Rudi.

Then it seemed as if Steven's knees buckled. *He's going to do it now*, Rudi thought. *This is his moment of glory.*

It was as if Marco had hypnotised him. Marco made him believe in a dream of endless girls. Every one of them wanting him.

Rudi tried crying out again, but his voice stuck in his throat.

Suddenly Steven was on all fours on the rigging.

He had lost his nerve.

His eyes moved across the crowd below him.

'Boo!' the kids now shouted. 'Boo!'

Rudi heard guys saying words like:

'Quitter!'

'Coward!'

'Chicken!'

But he didn't care.

Relieved, he watched as Steven made his way down the rigging. His hands seemed to tremble.

At last he was safely back on stage. He seemed confused.

Marco watched him with contempt. He spat on the ground before Steven.

Steven tucked at his white T-shirt. He stared at the crowd. They were still booing.

He dropped his head with embarrassment.

The cameras were still on him. Hundreds of them.

Rudi hurt inside. Steven looked so lost. It was his so-called friends jeering him. The girls who were supposed to like him.

As if spurred on by the noise, Steven raised his head. He was suddenly brimming with life again.

He gave a silly laugh.

Then he dashed off. Heading to the edge of the stage.

He launched himself at the crowd. It was a desperate leap. His body stretched out. He threw himself at the mercy of the onlookers.

They had to catch him, carry him on their hands.

That is how stage diving works.

But the guys and girls just stepped away.

Steven dropped like a sack of potatoes at their feet.

The power of words

The following day Rudi wandered around at home like a zombie.

He was glad the night was over. He never wanted to relive it again.

He thought about Steven. He wanted to send him a text.

Phoning him would actually be best. But he wouldn't know what to say.

The whole experience left a bad taste in his mouth.

He hoped Steven had learned his lesson.

Marco was a … well, a snake. He used people.

HI BUDDY, HOW ARE YOU TODAY?

Rudi sighed. He didn't finish typing. Instead he deleted the message before sending it.

'Talk to the guy,' he said to himself.

He searched for Steven's number and phoned.

'Hi, buddy … '

'Hi, Rudi.' Steven's voice was dark.

'I phoned to find out … uhm … ' Rudi stuttered. 'Are … you okay?'

Of course not! Jeez, Rudi, are you as stupid as mud? he told himself off.

'I'll probably live,' Steven answered.

'Wow, you sound a bit down.'

'Oh, well.'

Rudi's grip around the mobile phone felt cold. He should've sent a text instead. It would've avoided this terrible silence.

'So, what are you up to?'

'Lying about. Thinking. You know … ' Steven sighed.

Rudi felt more uncomfortable. He wished he could say something that would cheer Steven up. He didn't exactly know what. Anything. But even before he could say something, Steven started talking.

'Did you see the videos, Rudi?'

'No … '

'You should see what they're saying about me … '

The words were like ice water falling over Rudi.

'Is it … bad?'

'Go see for yourself … '

The conversation had reached its end.

Rudi ended the call. He quickly went onto YouTube, searching for the Vidiots videos.

There were tons of them. Of course the first ones, he had shot. The fire-crackers, the mousetraps, the snake …

But most of them were of last night.

Rudi held his breath. He didn't really want to watch them. It would force him to relive the evening.

But he knew he had to watch.

He felt sick after seeing the first video in the list.

Steven, the Loser! read the heading.

The shaking image showed Steven high above the stage.

The camera zoomed in, then out.

Steven's face was terror struck. Eventually he climbed back down, shaking. Uncertain of himself, he hung around on the stage. Then came the desperate stage dive …

The people laughing.

'Lame-O!' a voice shouted.

'Hammer head!' cried another one.

Rudi stopped the video. He didn't want to

hear the other remarks. But then his eyes fell on the comments below the video.

'The Vidiot dropped like a fly.'
'Perhaps he should keep to setting off fire-crackers.'
'The idiot cracked me up.'
'No more bad TV programs for you. It rots your brain, old Steven.'
'Pathetic!'
'Poor old stick!'
'How the mighty fall.'
'Ouch! Hope he didn't land on a mouse trap.'
'Why did the Vidiot run screaming from a haunted house? He was a scaredy pants!'

Rudi closed the screen.
There were more comments.
But he had seen enough.

Revenge is sweeter
when the blood flows

Rudi was furious. Nobody treated his pal this badly.

He wanted to kill Marco!

If he could only get his hands on him …

Marco wasn't a snake – he was *lower* than a snake.

Rudi phoned Lizz: 'Do you know where he is?'

'Who?'

'Marco, Lizz!'

'I don't know, Rudi. He goes to the gym in the afternoon ... '

Rudi ended the call. That was all he needed to hear.

His blood was boiling.

Lizz was spot on. Rudi caught up with him in front of the gym. He was just leaving.

Determined, Rudi approached Marco.

Marco raised his head. Frowned.

'Do you know what you did?' Rudi shouted. He pushed against Marco's shoulder.

'Hey, dude. Chill! What's up with you?' asked Marco.

'I'll show you!' Rudi grabbed Marco's helmet from his hands. He tossed it aside. The gym bag too.

Rudi's hand curled up into a fist.

'It's about time somebody rearranged your face,' growled Rudi. His attitude was threatening.

Marco pulled back his shoulders. He puffed his chest out. The corner of his mouth curled into a smile.

'And are you going to try, Rudi? Won't you get SCARED? I might hit back, dude.'

'Pig!' Rudi pulled his fist past his shoulder. His fingers were curled up tightly.

It was as if something inside him erupted. A volcano of anger.

The blow struck the side of Marco's head.

The pain shot through Rudi's fingers. Marco was seemingly hurt too.

But not enough.

He grabbed Rudi's shirt front. Pulled him closer. Rudi stared right into his fist. The white knuckles.

It came closer. He tried to pull away but the blow struck him against the eye.

He felt the skin tear. Then the blood came. It ran into his eyes.

Another blow hit him hard.

Rudi swore. He began striking back wildly.

The volcano's fire flared high inside him,
fists felt numb from all the blows. His knee
bore into Marco's ribs.

'And this one is for Lizz!' cried Rudi,
delivering another one. 'I know you're going to
hurt her as well!'

'Lizz? What do I care about her?' hissed
Marco. 'There are loads of girls out there. I
can get any one of them.'

'But not her!'

Rudi's knee struck Marco in the stomach.
Marco groaned.

Rudi pushed him to the floor. Marco was
under his feet. Rudi aimed a kick, but a hand
grabbed him.

'Stop it!' the security officer cried. More
people stormed out of the gym. 'Stop!'

Through bloodied vision Rudi stared at the
people. The security officer pushed Rudi and
Marco apart.

Rudi's T-shirt was covered in blood.

He didn't care.

He would've done it again for Steven.
And for Lizz.

War wounds

That evening Rudi looked in the bathroom mirror. His fingers gently touched the cut above his eye.

Ouch!

It still hurt.

One of his teeth felt loose too. He tried it. Yes, definitely loose. He considered pulling the tooth. He could just get a good grip on it …

No, he shivered. *Not now*.

Rudi stretched his back. His whole body felt stiff.

He wasn't a fighter. Every cell in his body knew it.

He wasn't used to this at all.

But he was glad he'd done it.

He'd had to!

He sat down on the edge of the bath and phoned Lizz.

She didn't answer.

Strange. Lizz always answered her mobile phone.

Later, in his bedroom, he tried again. There was still no answer.

Was it because he'd ended their other, earlier call abruptly? Perhaps he *had* been a bit cold with her.

Or was it because of Marco?

Rudi didn't have to wonder much longer.

His phone beeped.

I NEVER WANT TO TALK TO YOU
AGAIN. YOU WENT TOO FAR
TODAY.

It *was* about Marco.

Jeez, he just didn't understand girls. He
thought about calling her. Yelling at her:
*Can't you see, Liz? Marco is rubbish. Please open
your eyes.*

But Rudi didn't. He only texted back.

THINK AGAIN. MARCO SAYS THERE
ARE MANY GIRLS LIKE YOU. HE
COULD HAVE ANY ONE OF THEM.

Rudi lay on his bed.
He waited for a reply from Liz.
It didn't come.

A fist in the stomach

Monday morning. Rudi's bag was tight on his shoulder as he entered the school yard.

The stage was still set up on the rugby field. *They will probably pull it down later today*, he thought.

He dropped his bag at the English class. He looked the other bags over. Lizz and Steven's bags were already there. But *they* weren't.

His eyes moved across to the other kids.

He heard somebody talking about Zombie. The rock band. And Saturday evening.

Apparently the band had sung a few controversial songs.

The head master wasn't happy.

A few of the other guys were discussing the Vidiots.

That too had put the head master in a rage.

Rudi didn't follow the whole conversation. He was tired of it. It was a thing of the past.

Near the school hall he saw Lizz standing with Steven. Lizz had her arm around his shoulder. She was having a serious discussion with Steven. Every now and again he shook his head.

It felt like a fist had settled in Rudi's stomach.

Was Steven crying?

He still wasn't over those videos. And the terrible comments.

Who wants to be called a loser?

Steven wasn't a loser. Rudi knew it. He'd only done some stupid stuff to impress the girls.

Rudi stepped closer. But before he could reach them, Steven wiped off the tears and strode away.

Lizz dropped her arms helplessly.

Then she saw Rudi watching her.

Her eyes were void of emotion.

With lowered head, she walked off.

Rudi didn't know who to follow.

Steven? Or Lizz?

Or neither?

He decided on the last option.

The worry, however, remained.

He went back to the English class and found a seat at the front.

Deep in thought, he dug his prescribed book out of his bag. They were to write a test that morning and he hadn't studied for it.

He scanned the page.

But his thoughts were elsewhere.

Just as the bell was about to ring, something yanked Rudi out of his daydream.

It was a voice.

'Come check it out!' the guy cried. 'The Vidiot's going to attempt another jump!'

The smell of blood

No! The sound screamed inside Rudi.

A few guys pushed off in the direction of the voice.

Rudi knew he should follow them, but he was scared. What would he find when he got there?

The voice most likely came from the stage. It was still set up. That's probably where Steven had gone to.

It was as if somebody else moved inside Rudi's body. He got up. Started walking. Like someone lost.

Slowly at first.

Then with more determination.

Behind him the school bell rang out.

He ignored it.

A few of the kids turned back.

But others, like Rudi, didn't pay any attention to the bell.

It was as if they'd smelled blood.

They wanted to see it.

They wanted to say they were there.

They wanted to say how it was.

Use words like COOL. And GROSS. And AMAZING.

But would they record it too?

Rudi's head felt like it was at a standstill. Only his feet moved. Only his heart beat.

At the very top of the rigging Steven rose. His hands covering his eyes.

Rudi heard him cry.

'Are you going to jump this time?' one of the guys shouted.

'Shut up!' exclaimed Rudi. 'Can't you see what's happening? Do you want to encourage it?'

Rudi had reached the stage now. 'Get the high jump mattresses,' he quickly ordered one of the guys.

Then he began climbing.

His hands were sweating.

He was afraid.

What if he couldn't stop Steven?

Never doubt, never dread

Rudi reached the last rung. He pulled his body over the edge of the rig. It had a narrow metal walkway.

No decent place to hold on to.

The top of the rig was high above ground.

It hadn't *seemed* that high on Saturday evening. But then again, it had been dark. Now everything lay bright in the morning sun.

Lizz stood amongst the gathering crowd.

She stared up at them. She looked scared.

'Steven, what's up, buddy?' Rudi asked. His voice was trembling.

He moved closer.

But he didn't want to go too close.

Steven might get frightened.

And then …

Rudi didn't even want to think about it.

'I'm done, Rudi … with everything,' Steven said softly.

'Come on, bro. It's not that bad.'

'Don't come closer!'

Steven wiped his brow with his shirtsleeve. His face was red. His eyes were desperate.

That had changed too, Rudi realised. Saturday evening had been a dangerous adventure. But today was an all too real nightmare.

'I'm staying right here. Don't worry. We … we're simply going to talk. Don't you want you take a seat, Steven?'

'No!'

'Sit, Steven, please. Let's talk this thing through.'

'You don't know how bad I feel.'

'I think I know.'

'Rubbish! Nobody likes me. I had all those fans on YouTube … But I was their clown.'

'That's *their* problem. Not yours.' Rudi's mouth felt dry with tension. 'You're still the same guy. *I* know you. *I'm* your friend.'

'Rudi, stop the psychology lesson. Leave me alone!' Steven's eyes were fixed on the ground. His arms hung loose at his sides.

'I'm not going to leave you. Come with me. We can chat further on the ground. I'll buy you a Coke and a pie at the cafeteria.'

'The cafeteria is still closed,' Steven said in an emotional voice.

'I'll get them to open up. For you. And you'll see … next week … next month, we'll be laughing over this. The Vidiots was a stupid idea. We shouldn't have started it.'

'Marco ... ' The word exploded on Steven's tongue. Like a fire-cracker.

'I know ... he egged you on. You would never have done all that stuff of your own accord.'

Rudi sighed. He didn't know what more there was to say.

From the corner of his eye he saw a movement. A high-jump mattress appeared at the pavilion store room. Four guys were carrying it. One at each corner.

Soon after, a second mattress appeared.

Steven mustn't see it, thought Rudi.

He tried to keep up the conversation. 'Do you remember ... '

Rudi's voice was thin. He would need to talk about any nonsense now. To divert Steven's attention.

'Do you remember when we were in primary school ... We said we would never grow up. We were always going to ride our bikes. Magnum ice-cream would always be tops.

We'd never fall for girls. To kiss one would be the grossest thing ever.'

The mattresses were approaching quickly now …

Rudi smiled. But the tension remained.

'You said you would puke … if a girl stuck her tongue in your mouth.'

Steven gave a slight smile. He looked at Rudi. For the first time.

Rudi could see the pain in his friend's eyes.

'But things changed, Steven. You and I now both like girls. And we love Ben & Jerry's ice cream. We've grown up some. And it's not too bad actually.'

Below them the boys were now stacking the high-jump mattresses.

'But sometimes, Steven … we hit these speed bumps … But we don't let it get us down. We go on.'

Then something broke in Steven's eyes. He turned his head away from Rudi.

'Why did you bring the mattresses?'

Rudi didn't answer. He kept jabbering on.
'Do you remember that song from Hot Head?
You like it, don't you?'

Rudi started humming the words. His voice
was way off tune.

Steven shifted away.

Away from the mattresses down below …

Rudi stepped closer. Carefully. He sang
louder.

> *Lose your pain!*
> *Lose your fear!*
> *Stand strong*
> *Intentions clear!*
> *Never doubt, never dread*
> *For those secret worries*
> *Are only in your head.*

'Rubbish!' Steven cried all of a sudden.

He shot a quick sideways glance at Rudi.

Then he tumbled forward.

The fall

Rudi cried out. He couldn't believe it. Steven was going to miss the mattress!

Rudi didn't need to think any further. He shot forward.

His hand reached out before him.

He grabbed.

His fingers barely holding on to Steven's collar.

He shifted his grip. Got a better hold.

Rudi's other hand was curled around a beam near his feet.

He pulled Steven closer.

Steven hung there, suspended between heaven and earth. Like a marionette.

Rudi gnashed his teeth. Steven was heavier than he thought!

A drop of sweat ran down Rudi's temple. It dropped to the ground. Made a shiny spot way down there.

He wouldn't be able to hang onto Steven for much longer.

The guys on the ground again moved the mattresses into place.

For the second time, Rudi tried heaving Steven up.

He needed to get him to the top. It would be the safest. He didn't know if the mattresses would be thick enough to block a fall from that height.

But suddenly Steven's shirt tore.

Rudi tried shifting his grip. Grabbing him again.

And he nearly managed too.

But the shirt tore even further. The weight tugged heavily at Rudi's fingers.

He felt his own grip on the rigging slip.

'No!' he cried.

His fingers tore open.

'No!'

Steven slipped from Rudi' fingers.

And Rudi lost his own grip.

Both of them plummeted down.

The wind rushed past Rudi's head. He swung his arms and legs wildly. His eyes scared.

He saw Steven hitting the mattress first.

'Aargh!'

Rudi crashed down beside him. He felt something snap in his shoulder.

But he was okay.

Steven was too.

The last scene

'Delete it! Immediately!' the head boy ordered the guys with the mobile cameras.

They stared at him sheepishly. But then they complied, deleting the videos.

Rudi slowly straightened up. He clasped his shoulder. His collar bone was broken. He knew the feeling. He had broken it before in rugby.

Steven sat with his head lowered.

'It's over, Steven,' said Rudi. 'Everything will be all right. You'll see.'

Steven raised his head.

A guilty look in his eyes.

'Sorry,' he said softly. 'I … didn't want to drag you down as well.'

'It's okay. That's what friends are for.' Rudi smiled. 'But don't try it again. Next time you're on your own.'

Lizz made her way to them. Lily was right on her heels.

They were both as white as sheets.

'Are you okay?' asked Lizz breathlessly.

'Brother?' asked Lily. 'Steven?'

Rudi and Steven both nodded.

'Oh, thank goodness,' sighed Lily. 'You guys!' She went up to Steven, slipped her hand around him.

'Wow, I thought we were about to have a funeral,' said Lizz. There was a shocked silence. 'Sorry, bad joke … '

Steven just raised his eyebrows. His gaze

shifted from Lizz to Lily. 'It's okay, I thought so too!' He gave a guilty laugh.

'We all probably thought so,' said Rudi.

His eyes caught Lizz's. He held her gaze. Moments long. It made his heart tumble.

Then a sudden noise sounded in the street. It broke the precious moment.

Their heads jerked around. A motorbike roared a few times. The guy in black was watching them. He shook his head. And closed his helmet.

'Marco!' said Lizz. Her face hardened. She crossed her arms. 'Creep!'

With a spinning back wheel, Marco pulled away. Stones flying.

'That's the last we'll see of him,' said Rudi.

Lizz smiled. 'You'll be glad, won't you?'

Of course! thought Rudi. *Now I can try again …*

Lizz stepped closer. She gently touched Rudi's broken shoulder. Then she caressed the cut above his eye.

'Perhaps it's time I gave you a chance, Rudi. You know I like rough guys. And with all these new war wounds …Who knows – you might even steal my heart … '

Rudi smiled broadly, despite the pain. 'Oh, I'm sure I will!' he answered.

'But … ' A naughty look played in her eyes.

'Oh, here comes the kicker,' teased Steven.

'You'd better keep up, boy,' Lizz said wickedly. 'I might look like a Hollywood princess. But I have a dark side! That's why I like the rough guys!'

Rudi couldn't help blushing.

Lizz bent forward, kissing the scar above his eye. Her lips were incredibly soft. Warm.

'See you after school, Rudi,' she whispered.

Fanie is a well-known South African children's author, and the winner of a number of literary awards. He writes in both Afrikaans and in English and some of his books have been published in both languages.

The Afrikaans version of Jump was awarded an ATKV children's book award in 2014.

Fanie currently lives in Bloemfontein in South Africa.